PUFFIN BOOKS

RAGING ROBOTS & UNRULY UNCLES

'Watch out, villains,' muttered Prudence. 'Two can play at that game. One bad robot deserves another!'

Out of spare radio parts, biscuit tins and old soup cans, milk-bottle tops, bent nails, wire and an old frying-pan, Prudence created the Nadger – a veritable demon of a robot – to send to her seven cousins in return for the sickly-sweet robot, called Lilly Rose Blossom, they had sent her.

Prudence and her cousins hoped that the robots would cause trouble in each other's home, but even they could not have guessed just how bad things would be!

Margaret Mahy's rollicking adventure speeds from chaos to disaster and back again as the two tyrannical robots fulfil the awful promise of their creators. A rib-tickling story, which will keep the reader chuckling to the very last page!

Margaret Mahy is a New Zealander who has been writing stories from the age of seven. She has been awarded the Carnegie Medal twice and the Esther Glen Award three times. She has two grown-up daughters, several cats, a large garden and thousands of books. She lives near Christchurch, South Island. Margaret Mahy's books for Puffin include *The Downhill Crocodile Whizz and other Stories* and *The Boy Who Bounced and other Magic Tales*.

Raging Robots
& Unruly Uncles

Margaret Mahy

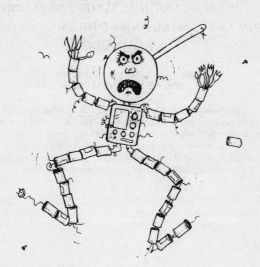

Illustrated by Peter Stevenson

Puffin Books

PUFFIN BOOKS

Published by the Penguin Group
Penguin Books Ltd, 27 Wrights Lane, London W8 5TZ, England
Penguin Books USA Inc., 375 Hudson Street, New York, New York 10014, USA
Penguin Books Australia Ltd, Ringwood, Victoria, Australia
Penguin Books Canada Ltd, 10 Alcorn Avenue, Toronto, Ontario, Canada M4V 3B2
Penguin Books (NZ) Ltd, 182–190 Wairau Road, Auckland 10, New Zealand

Penguin Books Ltd, Registered Offices: Harmondsworth, Middlesex, England

First published by J. M. Dent & Sons Ltd 1981
Published in Puffin Books 1985
7 9 10 8

Copyright © Margaret Mahy, 1981
Illustrations copyright © Peter Stevenson, 1981
All rights reserved

Printed in England by Clays Ltd, St Ives plc
Filmset in Monophoto Palatino

Contents

1

Uncle Jasper and his Seven Sons

Wicked Uncle Jasper was a villain by profession. He had seven sons, all boys, and all named after great villains of history — Caligula, Nero, Genghis, Tarquin, Belshazzar, Adolph and little Jack. Naturally their father wanted them to follow in his wicked footsteps and sent them to a very select School for Villains, but it was idle to pretend that they were doing at all well.

"What's this?" cried Uncle Jasper in horror as he read their school reports. "Caligula is at the bottom of the class in Despicable Treason, and though Nero is well up in Music he has totally failed in Utter Selfishness. Genghis — I hoped much from you, but your marks in Persecution are a disgrace and Tarquin, Tarquin — what can I say to a boy who has done so poorly in Cheating and Embezzlement. Belshazzar seems to be a dead loss at Robbery with Violence, and Adolph would be better at embroidery and stamp collecting than he is at Bribery and Corruption . . . . and as for little Jack — words fail me. You are bringing me grey hairs in sorrow to the grave."

(But this was just a poetic way of speaking as Jasper had no grey hairs that you'd notice, because he touched them up with a good brand of hair dye.)

"We do our best, Dad," said Caligula, "but it's all so boring."

"Not good enough!" Jasper cried, hitting the table with his riding crop. (He didn't go riding but he kept a good supply of riding crops around the house especially for hitting the table with whenever he lost his temper.) "That's not good

7

enough, Caligula. I've worked hard to send you to that school. Oh, the widows and orphans I've ground (when I could get any)! Oh, the state secrets I've sold (if I could lay my hands on them)! I've worn my fingers to the bone – to the bone I tell you — with Assault and Battery day in, day out, morning, noon and night. And now – now you tell me that Villainy is boring! Great Grommetting Wanglers!'' (for he was given to terrible swearing and cursing). ''Suppose Ivan the Terrible or Richard the Third had said it was boring and just given up? No villains! No villains at all! Nothing but heroes! Do you want that, hey? No darkness, only light! No balance, boy, no balance! Talk about *boring*.''

There was a guilty silence among the boys. They did not want to disappoint their father but there was no way out of it – they were all bored with Villainy. Genghis, who loved learning and scholarship, said, ''Actually, Father, there seems to be a lot of doubt whether Richard the Third *was* such a villain after all. You see, the history books of the time were written by his enemies, so, naturally. . . .''

''Don't try to confuse me with your academic quibbles, '' howled Jasper. ''Do you want to wind up as a University lecturer or even a teacher? I'd never shout at you again if you did that. No! I've made up my mind. You shall go to a special class on Black Magic that's being run by the Witches' Action Group every Saturday morning. That ought to ginger you up and it's bound to come in useful some time.''

The boys groaned and moaned but actually when they came to do their lessons they quite enjoyed them, and did a family project for the Shadows and Simulacra part of the course. They made a doll out of wax and enchanted it so that it seemed to be alive.

Even Jasper was intrigued. "You've done well, boys," he said grudgingly. "I suppose it's a beginning. Why did you have to make it so pretty though? It looks all sort of worthy and virtuous. It looks just like a heroine of the old-fashioned sort, and you know I can't stand them."

"When we were making it Genghis put a lot of the wrong stuff in," Caligula explained. "We were supposed to put in a teaspoonful of Naughtiness and he put in a tablespoonful of Nobleness. It's made a lot of difference."

"You know I'm short-sighted," grumbled Genghis.

"Well, I don't want it around here!" declared Jasper. "It reminds me too much of my brother Julian. It's just the way he would like your cousin Prudence to be."

"Hey Dad," said Nero eagerly, "I've got a good idea. Let's send this doll to Cousin Prudence as a present. Being a present they couldn't send it back, and it might stir up a lot of trouble one way and another."

"There you are, boys!" cried Jasper, a sudden gleam of hope in his tired eyes. "Nero has had a good idea! It's very gratifying. One battles on doing the best one can for one's children and then, just as one is losing hope – voilà! – things begin to drop into place. We'll buy some wrapping-paper with roses on it and twenty metres of pink ribbon."

"Ugh! Roses! Ugh! Pink ribbon!" cried the boys, who had been specially taught at their select school to detest roses and pink ribbon.

"Never mind, lads. The end justifies the means!" Jasper replied. "I have a feeling that this sickly doll is going to prove a thoroughly worth-while source of discomfort and misery to your cousin Prudence and her father, my virtuous twin brother Julian."

2

Julian and his Daughter Prudence

Jasper's twin brother – the virtuous Julian – lived with his only daughter Prudence on the other side of the city. They did not have much to do with the villainous side of the family, just sending them cards at Christmas and birthdays to keep in touch. (Jasper, of course, scorned to send Christmas cards, though he did send the occasional page of Foul Abuse which he was good at, or sometimes a begging letter on the off-chance.)

Whereas Jasper's wife, who had always planned to redeem him from his wicked ways through the love of a good woman, had gone off to join the army soon after little Jack was born, and risen rapidly to the rank of Sergeant Major, Julian's wife had, sadly, died. Being the only parent of an only daughter was a grave responsibility for Julian who was not sure of the rules. Different people told him different things. When Prudence grew up, berry brown, beanpole thin and needle-sharp, and often forgot to brush her tangled mouse-brown hair, he was sure he'd gone wrong somewhere. Worried about the taint of Villainy in the family, he enrolled her at the select Academy for Old-fashioned Heroines, a vegetarian school for girls. However, even this did not seem to be meeting the case. It was an anxious father who looked at Prudence's school report, and worried about her future, while Prudence (who already knew she was going to be a designer of computers and not an old-fashioned heroine) sat calmly buttering her toast.

"Look at this report, Prudence. You've got an A for reading – well, that's very good I don't deny – but you're only

average in Universal Benevolence. I'm glad to see you're well up in Hope, but you're well down in Faith and Charity. Now Prudence, you can't have one without the other two. The examiners won't even let you sit the exam. What's this? Your teacher has marked you down in Sense of Humour for going a great deal too far. Never forget that 'too far' is just as bad as 'not far enough'. Good gracious! Nearly bottom of the class in Lofty Sentiments and completely bottom of the class in Self Denial and Bitter Remorse."

"Well, I haven't got much to be remorseful about," Prudence said.

"A good heroine – especially the old-fashioned, reliable kind – always has something to feel remorseful about," Julian said reprovingly.

"O.K. I'll have a go at feeling remorseful about not feeling remorseful," said Prudence with the ghost of a chuckle.

Julian looked at her doubtfully and then back at her report.

"You've done well in Fair Play," he admitted, "but you can't build a whole career around sport. Oh yes – top marks in Electronics. I'm not too impressed with that, Prudence."

"Why not?" asked Prudence rather indignantly. "I've mended the television set twice this week and it would have cost a whole lot of money if we'd had to have someone in to fix it."

She wished her father wouldn't worry so much about her character. Having a villain for a twin brother made him very jumpy and he kept watching for signs of wickedness. He himself, if he'd been going to Worried Fathers' School, would have got 100 per cent in Anxiety.

At that moment there came a knock at the door. It was the postman with a very large parcel wrapped in paper printed with roses and tied up with great lengths and loops of pink string.

"Look at this!" cried Julian. "It's a present from wicked

Uncle Jasper and the bad cousins."

"For me?" Prudence asked. "I'll bet it explodes. Let's send it back straightaway, or get someone else to open it."

"Perhaps they've had a change of heart," Julian said hopefully.

"Perhaps pigs might fly," said Prudence rather sourly, but she couldn't help being really curious and pulled off the string which seemed to go on for ever, folded the paper back carefully and opened the box inside. It was full of tissue paper with a card tucked in on top.

"Dear Prudence," said the card. "We hope you have hours of fun with this Walkie-Talkie doll."

"For heaven's sake!" exclaimed Prudence. "A walkie-talkie doll! It's an insult all right! A walkie-talkie doll. At the very least they could have called it a robot!" But her cries of outrage were cut short. The tissue paper stirred and out of its snowy foam rose a tall figure – almost as tall as Prudence but much more delicate – with feathery golden curls, big blue eyes and long eyelashes. It was wearing a blue dress with a frill around the bottom, and a white muslin apron with a frill around the edge and a pretty pocket with a crisp little blue handkerchief peeping out. It had white socks and new blue shoes and smiled at Uncle Julian and Prudence with a smile like pink candy floss. Then it spoke in a voice that sounded as if it had been eating golden syrup.

"Hello, Uncle Julian. Hello, dear Prudence. My name is Lilly Rose Blossom and I've come to play, and to stay, with best wishes from Caligula, Nero, Tarquin, Genghis, Belshazzar, Adolph and little Jack."

"It *is* a robot and it means trouble," thought Prudence. "That set of sharks wouldn't do a dog a good turn. They haven't got any kindness of heart between the lot of them. In fact, I don't expect they even *do* Kindness of Heart at Villains' School. I'll have to watch out, I can see that."

But it was plain that Julian was very impressed with Lilly

Rose Blossom who looked like his idea of an old-fashioned heroine. Sure enough, when they sat down to dinner Prudence's worst fears were realized. They were eating a rather thin soup made with paragons and quite tasteless unless you put in plenty of the salt of the earth.

Prudence herself was not a very tidy eater of soup. Her head was always full of thoughts and dreams, not table manners, and as usual she splashed it on to the table-cloth.

"Prudence," said Uncle Julian, "you are slurping your nutritious paragon soup again. Lilly Rose Blossom is eating *beautifully*, and she is only a doll. Here is a glass of the milk of human kindness. Don't spill any, for it is hard to come by."

Later he was heard to say, "Prudence, Lilly Rose Blossom has eaten all her paragons. Surely you – a live girl with a human conscience – can do the same."

And later still, "Prudence, Lilly Rose Blossom has washed the dishes, dried the dishes and put them away. She has wiped down the bench and tidied the cupboard under the sink until it is a model of what an under-the-sink cupboard ought to be. And all you've done is to sit there reading a book about computers. It's not good enough."

Prudence was willing to admit that she was not all she might be when it came to helping around the house, but it was irritating being compared unfavourably with a doll.

Later Lilly Rose Blossom went straight to bed with a saintly smile and no grumbling or begging for just ten

minutes more television. Prudence lay in the dark, scowling and hissing like a boiling kettle.

"O.K. So that's what they're up to, is it? O.K.! They're *for* it! Watch out Caligula, Nero, Tarquin, Genghis, Belshazzar, Adolph and little Jack! You have brought doom and destruction upon yourselves."

Next morning Lilly Rose Blossom ate her Humility Porridge without a word of complaint and then tidied up Prudence's electronics magazines without being asked to. She behaved as if she would have got 100 per cent with no trouble at all, in Benevolence and Lofty Sentiments. No wonder Julian looked at her with a fond eye, thrilled to have someone in his midst behaving like an old-fashioned heroine, even if it was only a doll.

Lilly Rose Blossom's voice was sweet and her smile was so full of candy floss that Prudence found the whole house becoming sticky with sweetness, especially the door-handles and window-ledges, though Julian did not seem to notice this. It became so sugary that Prudence carried her electronics box and her notebooks out into the garage where she straightaway began inventing.

"Watch out, villains!" she muttered. "Two can play at

that game. One bad robot deserves another.''

Out of spare radio parts, biscuit tins and old soup cans, milk-bottle tops, bent nails, wire and an old frying-pan, Prudence had soon made a rather dreadful doll of her own – more of a robot than a doll really, powered by an assortment of batteries.

Concealed in the back of the robot was a dial drawn on cardboard with a wire needle. When it was turned off, the needle pointed to PERFECT VIRTUE. In these circumstances the robot just stood there, doing nothing and saying nothing. But when it was switched on and the batteries were working, the wickedness circuits were activated and the needle crept around from CARELESS, to DOWNRIGHT INCONSIDER-ATE, on to BAD, to VILLAINOUS, to SUPERVILLAINOUS – and *then* the robot behaved like a veritable demon!

In the very box which had once held Lilly Rose Blossom, Prudence folded her invention, tied it up in rosy paper, looped it to the point of extinction with pink ribbon, and looked at the parcel with satisfaction.

''The cousins in opposition!'' she muttered gleefully. ''Let them try *that* one for size.''

Life was going to be rather miserable for a while, she thought as she carried her parcel down to the Post Office. A lot of her favourite radio parts were gone (used up on the robot) and inside the house Lilly Rose Blossom was spreading sugar everywhere, but Prudence was prepared to put up with it for a little bit longer. She hoped that, when the robot really got going, the bad cousins would come and take Lilly Rose Blossom away.

3

A Present from Prudence

Jasper and his boys were nonplussed when the big parcel covered in roses, looped with pink ribbon, was delivered back to them the following day.

"I didn't think that goody-goody Julian would return it unopened," said Jasper in a discontented voice. "Do you suppose the magic has worn off? Open it, Belshazzar, and let's check up on it."

"That particular sort of magic is supposed to be permanent unless you say the counter-spell," Caligula said in a puzzled voice.

They were astonished when, out of the crumpled tissue paper, there arose a figure of tin, wire, bent nails and bottle-tops. It was topped by a round frying-pan on which was a face – a face with a rusty hole for a mouth and with its eyes and nose drawn on with blue felt-pen. It had a curious, surprised expression that was also very creepy indeed. Out of the rusty hole came a voice.

"I am the Nadger!" it announced, sounding like shrieking hinges, long finger-nails being scraped down a blackboard, and bones being gnawed by strong yellow teeth. "I am a gift from Cousin Prudence. Get lost, the lot of you!"

"Crumbling Malediction!" exclaimed Jasper, delighted by the creature's insolence and repulsive appearance. "Now *that's* something like!"

"Shall we kick it to pieces?" asked Jack, for the bright little fellow was anxious to win his father's approval.

"Just try it," creaked the Nadger, "and I'll fillet you."

Jasper was enchanted all over again. "We'll think about

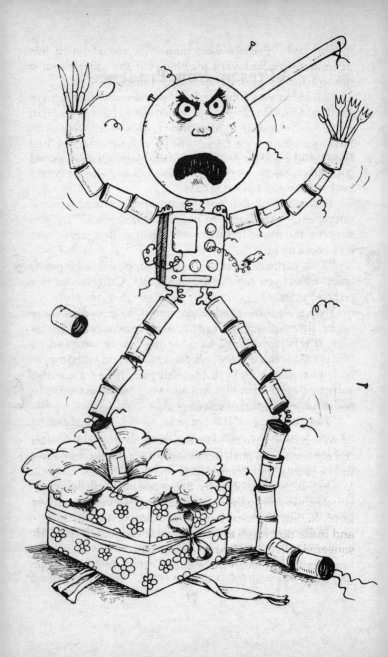

it," he said. "Perhaps after dinner we can all shred this perambulating junk-yard together. On the other hand, it doesn't do to be too hasty over these things."

"I'll shred you!" the Nadger said, like an angry echo of itself, and aimed a blow at Jack which would have caused him grave discomfort if it had landed. However, what with having a villain for a father and six older brothers he had become very good at dodging, and the blow merely shattered a kitchen chair.

When they were all seated around the table, the Nadger did not hesitate to push Belshazzar off his chair and sit down in his place. Belshazzar leaped up, doubling his fists but, looking at the knobbly wiry figure and meeting the astonished expression on the frying-pan face (the eyes were drawn in on slightly different levels) he unclenched his fists again and made do as well as he could with the broken chair. He squeezed in between Tarquin and Genghis who both elbowed him painfully, though more out of conscientiousness than real spite.

The meal was home-made Hooligan Pie with Barbarity Sauce and plentiful helpings of peccadillos and shenanigans, followed by Delinquency Pudding smothered with honeyed lies and sprinkled with Fraud.

"Tarquin – what's this?" asked Jasper in pained tones. "You're not eating your peccadillos."

"They're too hard to swallow," Tarquin complained. "They're like tall stories."

"Ha!" sneered Jasper. "Look at the Nadger! He's eaten *all* his peccadillos and some of Nero's shenanigans as well. He doesn't muck around with his food like *you*, you lazy lay-abouts."

The Nadger was wiping the last crumbs of Fraud from around his rusty mouth. Then with a single sweep of his arm he sent his dish spinning across the room to shatter against the wall. Little did the brothers realize that special consumption units were breaking the food down into molecules somewhere inside him and producing chemical energy to recharge his batteries.

"Great Spangling Clodwinkles!" swore Jasper. "He's got style, that Nadger. I like to see it," and he gave a great roar of laughter. However, a moment later his good humour left him.

23

"Adolph! Genghis! Where are you skulking off to?"

"Well Dad — well — we've run out of dishes," Genghis stammered. "I thought I'd just rinse a few — not wipe down the bench or anything like that, of course — just get most of the grease off some of the dishes. . . . " He broke off, for Jasper was swelling alarmingly, even foaming at the mouth a little, twirling his moustache in a very ecstasy of villainous fury. The Nadger emitted a short bark of contemptuous sound that could have been a laugh.

"Genghis — do you or do you not take Unimaginable Squalor as a subject at school?" Jasper demanded.

"Yes, Dad," Genghis admitted, "but lots of villains lead lives of unimaginable luxury on their ill-gotten gains. You don't *have* to put up with dirty dishes, you know. It's not compulsory."

"You don't have to behave like a damned housemaid either," roared his father. "I'd have sent you to Housemaids' College if that's what I had in mind for you. I want you to be a villain, boy, a VILLAIN."

Jasper seized Genghis and banged him against the wall a few times. "I'm not doing this for personal pleasure, you know. I'm fond of you, and it's for your own good. Do the dishes indeed! Why, I bet that Nadger knows what to do about dirty dishes better than you do."

The Nadger took this as an invitation and set off eagerly into the kitchen with a rattling, ominous stride. A moment later loud smashings and crashings were heard as he threw the dishes to the floor one at a time. Even Jasper's fine snarl wavered uncertainly as the smashing went on and on. . . . and on. . . . and on. . . .

"I suppose you realize," said Caligula, giving his father a very promising sneer, "that that animated collection of tin cans has thrown a seventy-six piece dinner service piece by piece on to the floor — a wedding present of yours, I seem to remember you telling me."

"Malevolence!" cried Jasper scornfully. "If I'd remembered that I'd have broken it long ago. And Caligula — remember, when you sneer at me, to curl your lip more. Don't leave anyone in doubt as to what you're doing. You don't want people to think you've merely got a nervous twitch."

The Nadger stalked out of the kitchen and went to the dining-room door.

"Where do you think you're going?" Jasper cried.

"Steal more dishes!" the Nadger replied, swivelling its horrid, holey frying-pan head in Jasper's direction. "Burgle a china shop!"

Jasper was delighted. "Stab my vitals!" he exclaimed. "It's nice to have a twin soul in the house at last. Blow me if I don't go and brush up on a bit of Car Conversion, just to keep my hand in. And you lot — why don't you get out and practise a bit of Pick-pocketing and Pilfering. Genghis could do with a lot of practice."

"Jasper! Dad!" Caligula said, "you've touched upon a difficult topic."

"What?" Jasper halted and stared at his sons.

"Well, we had a sight test at school today, and I'm afraid to tell you that Genghis is noticeably short-sighted, and is certainly going to need glasses."

Jasper leaped as if stung (though not, of course, by remorse).

"Glasses? *Glasses*, you say? How can he hope to be a villain in glasses? He's not getting glasses, and I'm telling you that right now!"

"I might be better with glasses," Genghis suggested in a desperate voice. "I could be one of those deadly, clean-shaven, weedy little villains with rimless glasses. I *need* glasses. When I had to read a piece on Moral Turpitude at school I kept making mistakes."

"He kept on saying 'moral turpentine' and making every-one laugh," Adolph explained.

Jasper emitted a hoarse cry. "I've had enough. You're a spineless lot to begin with, but when I hear that you've been holding the profession of Villainy — the oldest profession in the world except for gardening — up to mockery and derision I could break down and cry like a child. I'd sooner have a family of Nadgers. The Nadger's got what it takes."

"It sounds as if it's going to take what other people have got," said Nero disapprovingly.

Jasper twirled his moustache. "Maledictions!" he swore. "Don't you bandy words with me or you'll regret it. Now listen, the lot of you! I'm going out to convert some cars and raise general mayhem and —" his voice took on a note of icy menace "— by the time I return I want you to have perpetrated some act of Villainy so monstrous that even the police, hardened to all manner of horrors, will talk of yours in hushed voices. You're all old enough to be getting into the big time."

"Can we do it between the seven of us?" asked Tarquin heavily.

"Or do we have to do one each?" asked little Jack.

"I'd be pathetically grateful for just one between the lot of you, you milksops," Jasper declared as he slammed out of the house, following the Nadger.

27

The boys looked at one another in silence.

"Well, frankly, that DOES it as far as I'm concerned," said Caligula. "I vote we run away — go tonight, straightaway, promptly, presto and apace. Steal his life-savings and then run away and try to break his poor old heart! See how he likes that!"

"All his life-savings?" asked Nero. "We'll never carry them all. His one-and-two-cent collection weighs about a ton."

"Just some of them," Caligula said. "Let's have a look in the Life-Savings Storeroom."

The life-savings were triple-locked in an old pantry where they were stored in glass jars like bottled fruit. But lock-picking was child's play to these boys, and they were soon reading the labels on the jars. . . . WIDOW AND ORPHAN-GRINDING, FORECLOSING MORTGAGES, BLACK-MAIL, FORGED WILLS and BOUNCING CHEQUES.

"Let's fill our pockets from that one," Tarquin advised.

"I'm taking some from STOLEN CLUB MONEY," little Jack declared.

"I'll have a bit from SALE OF STOLEN GOODS." Adolph levered the top off a particularly large jar.

They had actually often talked about running away. The appearance of the Nadger, and Jasper's particularly insulting behaviour, had merely hastened things for them a little bit.

4

The Runaways

The boys left immediately without encumbering themselves with so much as a change of clothes. They were anxious to be far away by the time Jasper returned, with or without the Nadger. Through the midnight streets they trudged, their faces now greenish under the ghastly gleam of each street lamp, now shadowed as they passed beyond its circle of power. They moved from light to dark, and dark to light again, like a troop of wandering magicians with uncertain magical powers.

There were many hoodlums and larrikins abroad in the night but the sight of seven boys with a basic training in all branches of Villainy made them shrink into doorways or fade into shadows.

At first they talked quietly among themselves but a little later, overwhelmed by the mystery and silence of the sleeping city, they sang a verse or two of their school song:

> The hot dog needs the mustard,
> The ice-cream needs the ice,
> If Life's a bowl of custard
> Then Villainy's the spice.
> Without a little wickedness
> To make a little stir
> How would the virtuous people
> Know how virtuous they were?

Chorus Villainy, oh Villainy, we carol in thy praise,
      Your apothogems and precepts we will practise all
        our days.

The sound of breaking promises
Is music to our ears,
We mock the Doubting Thomases
And justify their fears.
Embezzlement or Larceny
Our teacher will applaud,
We cheat in every class and he
Will praise us for the fraud.

Chorus   Villainy, oh Villainy, a study without peers,
Your edicts and enactments will be with us all our
      years.

There were twenty-six verses, but before they were half-way through they stopped in the shadows for, down the long dim street, a light was coming steadily towards them.

"It's someone on a bicycle," Belshazzar said.

"Perhaps we ought to attack them a bit," Adolph suggested but without any real enthusiasm.

"Oh don't let's bother," muttered Tarquin. "We're not at school now. It's a sort of holiday really."

The bicycle came purposefully onward, obviously pedalled by very competent feet, considering the lateness of the hour. Then the rider suddenly saw them clustered in the gloom and the cycle came to a rattling, unexpected stop.

"Good heavens! It's Caligula — and Nero — and all the wicked cousins," the bicycle rider said.

"It's Prudence!" exclaimed Caligula. "It's goody-goody Prudence." He immediately started to accuse, as villains are trained to do. "I suppose you realize this is all your fault. That Nadger you sent us has driven us out of the home of our childhood."

"It wasn't the home of your childhood," said Prudence scornfully. "Do you think I don't know that you've lived in about fifty different homes and that you always leave without paying the rent? And anyway, what about that Lilly Rose Blossom you sent me? You started it, didn't you, with Lilly Rose Blossom? She's absolutely unbearable, simpering all over the place, tidying up my electronics magazines. I've just had to run away, that's all."

"Funny!" said Nero. "Isn't that funny, Caligula?" And all seven brothers exclaimed in one not-so-very-villainous chorus, "We've run away too."

Prudence was silent for a moment. In the greenish glow of the street light they could see her smile an unwilling smile.

"Shall we have a midnight party and talk this over?" she suggested. "I've biked a long way and I feel like refreshments."

"Good idea!" Caligula said, "though there are no shops open at this hour of night. We'll have to steal something."

"No need!" Prudence replied. "I've got lots of sandwiches."

They were close to a scrap-metal yard (which looked like the end of the world as such businesses often do) filled with pieces of tin, rusting bicycles, oil-drums, old car bodies and bits of roofing iron. Among them was an ancient bus, and into this the cousins climbed for their midnight feast. From her backpack Prudence took huge packets of sandwiches.

"All good straightforward food — nothing with a moral," Prudence declared. "Cold roast beef and horseradish sauce

31

in here," she said. "Lettuce and tomato in this one, hard-boiled egg, mayonnaise and chives in here, and plain ham in this bundle. I brought a lot because I get very hungry at home so I've plenty to share. I don't mind if we eat it all either. Something else will turn up."

There was dead silence while the first round of sandwiches was eaten.

"That's the most delicious thing I've ever eaten in all my life," Adolph said with a sigh as he finished his first sandwich.

"It's the *only* delicious thing I've ever eaten," said little Jack. "It's a hundred times nicer than Hooligan Pie, and a thousand times nicer than peccadillos."

"Is that what you have?" Prudence asked curiously. "You should try paragons — or rather you shouldn't. They're almost totally tasteless — really dreary, and somehow they make everything else taste dreary too."

"At our school they sometimes give us Dudgeon," Belshazzar took another two sandwiches, "but it's nearly always high, and it tastes horrible."

"At *my* school they sometimes have Comfort," Prudence sighed. "It sounds very nice but they take a long time to serve it and it's always cold. And at home it's worse, and that horrible doll you sent me laps up paragon soup and asks for more."

"Your robot ate my shenanigans," Nero said. "Not that I minded." There was silence while the cousins stuffed themselves with more delicious sandwiches.

"What are you running away to?" asked Prudence at last. "You haven't brought much with you."

"Oh, we'll steal what we need as we go," Belshazzar explained. "We've all done Basic Banditry and Highway Robbery. What about you?"

"Oh I've got an honest trade," Prudence said, rather snootily. "I'm not going to go running around hiding from shadows and policemen. I'm going to repair television sets

and stereos. I can, you know.''

''Who's going to trust a girl of your age with their expensive television set?'' asked Adolph sarcastically. ''One look at you and they'll shut their doors and yell, 'Come back when you're fifteen years older and have turned into a man'.''

''I may have a bit of a problem there,'' Prudence said gloomily, ''but I'll just have to try. I don't want to be a heroine,'' she added, ''particularly the old-fashioned sort. It's not a very good line of business.''

''But you've been trained to be an old-fashioned heroine,'' Caligula said, watching her keenly. ''Why not *be* one?''

''I just don't WANT to be one,'' Prudence replied.

''That's very interesting,'' said Caligula slowly, ''because I just don't *want* to be a villain, in spite of my training.''

''Nor me,'' agreed Nero.

''Our hearts aren't in it,'' added Tarquin and there were murmurs of agreement from the other four boys. Everyone looked at everyone else as if they had only just been introduced.

"I want to be an actor," said Caligula. "Acting was the one thing I did well at, at Villainy School. I got top marks."

"He got the highest marks ever awarded to anyone," Nero told Prudence, "and it was a tough exam too. He had to pretend he'd been arrested and persuade the policeman to let him go."

"Did he manage it?" asked Prudence, deeply interested.

"He was terrific!" Belshazzar cried. "The policeman was a special detective inspector brought in for the test from the Police Department. He was supposed to be very tough but when Caligula really got going on his hard-luck story, the Detective Inspector not only let him go, but wrote out a cheque for his entire life-savings and forced Caligula to accept it."

"It was a great triumph for the whole family," said Genghis. "Even our teacher was in tears. He organized a special collection to help Caligula before he realized what he was doing."

"He got A + + + + + + + which is the highest mark you can get," concluded little Jack and they all looked at Caligula proudly in the gloom.

"Do you all want to be actors?" asked Prudence.

"No, I want to be a chef," said Nero. "I *thought* I did, and since eating those roast beef and horseradish sauce sandwiches I know I want to work with food for the rest of my days. It was as if a piece of a jigsaw puzzle fitted into place. And you know, with all the beating up and chopping up and slicing and mashing there is in cooking, some of my villainy training will come in useful."

"Well, I suppose everyone will laugh at the idea," said Genghis, "but I want to be a librarian. I was a librarian at school and it was the only thing that kept me going. I catalogued the sections on Historical Villainy and Dramatic Explosions. But I'll have to get glasses first."

"You don't have to have glasses," Prudence said. "It isn't a library rule these days."

"Maybe not," Genghis said, "but you need to be able to read fine print. You see, I don't want to be one of those progressive librarians trying to make the library the centre of community life. I want to be one of those scholarly librarians working with old newspapers, diaries, and so on, tracing obscure facts and running mysterious dates to a standstill before they vanish for ever."

"Talking of family trees," Belshazzar remarked rather shyly, "I want to be a gardener. When I thought I was going to have to be a villain I wasn't too worried. I thought, well, I'm so bad at it I'm bound to get caught and then I'll try to get a job in the prison garden. I want to plough and sow and reap and hoe and water plants, and cut trees and hedges into beautiful shapes. I want to mow lawns and put the clippings on a really well-made compost heap and thin carrots and spray roses, and all that sort of thing."

"I want to be a bus driver," said Adolph, who was sitting in the driver's seat of the dilapidated bus. "I've only just thought of it but now that seems the thing I've always wanted to be. What about you, Tarquin?"

"I want to be a fortune-teller," Tarquin said, "I loved working with the tarot cards at our classes in Magic on Saturday morning, and I was never once wrong with the fortunes I foretold."

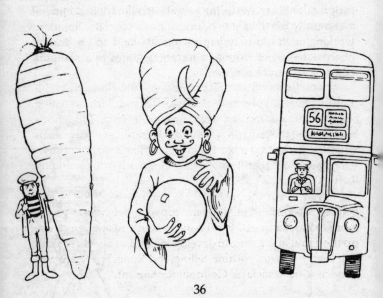

"What a funny mixture of things we want to do," said Prudence. "I wonder if we'll ever be able to do them."

"I don't see why not," said little Jack. "I don't see why we shouldn't do all these things together. Caligula can look quite grown up. Why doesn't he act the part of a businessman and rent a shop for Prudence, with a house for all of us at the back? Nero can cook our dinners and Belshazzar can make a garden for us. Caligula can go out and look at television sets and stereos, dressed as a Television and Stereo Repairman. He can make himself look old and responsible, and carry a big tool-kit with Prudence hidden in it. As soon as he's alone with the television set, he opens his tool-kit and out comes Prudence, fixes it and then gets back into the bag to be carried home again. And while Caligula and Prudence are out doing that, Tarquin can be at home telling fortunes, and Genghis can. . .he can. . .Genghis can do our research for us — checking out recipes, new sorts of gardening ideas, or even old ones that are nearly forgotten, or television things — whatever we need to know."

His brothers and Prudence stared at him.

"What will *you* do while all this is going on?" Caligula asked.

"I'll do the publicity and promotion," little Jack cried. "I'll draw posters saying 'Television Repair and Fortune-telling Service' and Adolph can whizz around town on Prudence's bike pasting them up on walls and telegraph poles. . . .Then when we can afford a bus it'll be Television Repair, Fortune-telling and Suburban Transport Service, with Adolph driving the bus."

"What about the restaurant?" cried Nero. "You're forgetting the restaurant. I mean, suppose Belshazzar grows more than we can eat. We'd have to start a restaurant to use up the extra, and for me to develop my skill as a cook. Make it Television Repair, Fortune-telling and Suburban Transport Service with Associated Gourmet Restaurant."

"Make it Television Repair, Fortune-telling and Suburban Transport Service with Associated Gourmet Restaurant and Market Garden," cried Belshazzar quickly.

"Make it Television Repair, Fortune-telling and Suburban Transport Service with Associated Gourmet Restaurant, Market Garden and Reference Library," Genghis hastily amended. "That gives it an intellectual touch. And I have some ideas for up-dating the library by using trained parrots."

"It's going to be a lot to put on one poster," grumbled little Jack, "but why not? Put it all on."

"We'd better get on with it," said Prudence. "What a piece of luck that we met! Shall we just ride around until we find a suitable place or what?"

"Can't!" said Genghis, "unless you let us steal a car — though mind you, we all got very poor marks at Car Conversion. Our hearts weren't in it. Once Tarquin actually left a letter of apology with his name and address on it."

"Could we get *this* bus working?" Adolph asked. "No one seems to need it." Prudence actually investigated the possibility for she was an expert with cars, but alas, it proved to have no motor and, as she told them, you can't repair what isn't there. However, there were fortunately many old bikes in various stages of disintegration, and it was but the work of

a moment — several moments — quite a lot of moments, in fact — for Prudence to use her skill and the available bits of bike, to put together a great long cycle with eight pairs of handlebars and nine wheels. Finally the nonocycle was ready, cleverly hinged in the middle for taking sharp corners.

"We'll just trundle around inconspicuously on our nonocycle keeping our eyes open for likely establishments," Prudence said. "You know, I think things are looking up. A new Era is dawning for us all (as they say at Heroines' School). No more paragon soup and cold Charity!"

"No more shenanigans and peccadillos," Caligula sighed with pleasure.

"No more moral turpentine," added Genghis.

"No more Cheating and Embezzlement," cried Tarquin. "Only Honest Labour. Shall we like it, do you think?"

"Bound to!" said Belshazzar, "because it's what we really want to do. No more Robbery with Violence."

"I'm never going to have to sit through Bribery and Corruption again," breathed Adolph. "I'd never have passed in a million years."

"Who knows — we may end up living happily ever after, after all," little Jack shouted hopefully, his voice echoing off the rubble in the scrap-metal yard.

Climbing on to the nonocycle they set off through the streets full of hope and sandwiches, looking for a suitable establishment, while in the sky above, the rosy fingers of dawn seemed to be drawing the curtain on a new scene, a new day.

"If ever we do get a restaurant," little Jack said, "let's paint it all pink like the sunrise to recall this glorious morning," and everyone on the nonocycle agreed.

What Happened to Julian, What Happened to Jasper

By the next morning it occurred to Jasper that his seven sons had run away.

"I do believe they're trying to break my poor old heart," he said gleefully, quite encouraged, for it is not uncommon for young villains to break their fathers' poor old hearts. (But of course anyone trying to break Jasper's poor old heart had their work cut out, and well he knew it.)

"I love 'em for trying," he chuckled to himself, "but they won't succeed. They'll come skulking home and find me as cheerful as a cricket. That'll teach them that successful Villainy isn't a pushover. It needs years of dedication. And while they're gone I'll have a high old time. Children do tend to clog a parent's initiative. I'd often like to relax but I feel I've got to lead the way for the boys, set an example and so on. Now I'll have a bit of a rest."

Jasper was quite philosophical about losing his seven boys.

Julian, on the other hand, was distraught to find that Prudence had run away. He sent for the police and within an hour the house was filled with detectives taking fingerprints and looking at things through magnifying glasses.

"Do you think you'll find her, my little girl?" he asked in a pathetic voice that made Prudence sound a lot smaller than she really was.

"As to that I couldn't say, sir," replied the cheerful policeman. "We do find some, and then others, they seem to vanish off the face of the earth. Depends where she's run to, of course. But we'll certainly have a good look round. And you *have* got a spare one, so you're not so badly off." He looked over to where Lilly Rose Blossom sat smiling and smoothing her spotless apron with spotless hands.

"Lilly Rose Blossom is a great comfort to me," said Julian, patting her golden curls.

But later that evening when the policeman and the detective had gone home to put their feet up — and to try and find Prudence by brainwork and deduction — Lilly Rose Blossom proved not to be such a comfort after all.

She came and stood by Julian's chair holding a fat book and saying, "Look at this volume of improving stories I found in the spare room, Uncle Julian. Will you please, PLEASE read me a few of them, dear Uncle Julian."

Now the books in the spare room bookcase were put there because they were too boring for anyone to enjoy, but too well-bound to throw away. This one was very old, but had been read so little it looked almost new, with its shiny brown binding and gold letters. It was called *One Thousand Improving Little Tales For Progressive Little Minds* by Nanny Gringe.

The print was very small. Prudence would never have taken it down from the spare room bookcase in a million years and she would rather have been stung by scorpions than had one of Nanny Gringe's inspiring tales read to her. She didn't want to be improved that much. Julian took the book, saying with a sad smile, "I don't think you need to be improved, Lilly Rose Blossom. I think you're practically perfect."

"Yes, but I like to hear an improving tale now and then," said Lilly Rose Blossom. "Just in case!" she added with her candy-floss smile. So poor Julian had to read six improving tales and they were terribly boring. The children in them were boring, and the improving bits were so boring that Julian wondered if they were really as improving as they were supposed to be. In spite of being sorely worried, he began yawning and nodding and did not feel improved in the slightest. He decided to go to bed early. But that wasn't much good, for just as he was dropping into a fitful slumber Lilly Rose Blossom appeared again with Nanny Gringe's book tucked under her arm.

"Poor Uncle Julian!" she said. "You were so good reading to me that I thought I'd say 'thank you' by reading to *you* for a little. It may help you to sleep."

"Thank you, my dear, I'm almost asleep already," replied the weary Julian, but she sat down in an implacable way saying,

"Well, it's true that I am practically perfect, but you could do with a lot of improvement, dear Uncle — if you don't mind me saying so, that is — so I'll do the reading from now on and you do the listening."

Then she read him seventeen improving stories, each one worse than the one before. If he began to go to sleep she had a way of clearing her throat that was very soft but also very threatening and he was forced to wake up and listen. The improving stories went on and on and on. Julian found

himself wishing that she would go off and do something else
— something useful and benevolent, but mainly something
ELSE — such as fixing a television set. He found he missed
Prudence in spite of her poor record at Heroines' School. And
he went on missing her. . . .

On the other side of town Jasper was taking things easy.
Indeed for the first few days of being without his boys he took
things very easy indeed. Then, after that, it suddenly became

a lot harder. He started off behaving in a very degenerate, deplorable fashion as villains often do when they are not involved in active wickedness. He slept until nearly two o'clock every afternoon, and then just slouched in bed reading racy stories, eating peppermint creams and slices of white bread and jam, and drinking fizzy wine. The Nadger, on the other hand, was on the move the whole time and when, after a week in bed, Uncle Jasper (having caught up with his reading and having finished the jam and the peppermint creams) staggered into his living-room, he was astounded at the change. For a moment he thought he had somehow wandered into a supermarket.

45

There was not only a complete dinner service in red china but there were seventy-six tins of cat food, fourteen tins of mahogany timber stain, innumerable ball-point pens, seven dozen eggs, two red floppy floor mops, a box of tinned fruit salad, and several cartons of ice-cream which was now totally melted. There were beer glasses, tubes of toothpaste, one hundred and two pairs of nylon stockings and other assorted underwear, fifteen TV dinners (mostly fish, which Jasper did not like), many tins of shoe polish (mainly black and mid-brown) as well as numerous other objects that it was difficult for Jasper to think of an immediate use for, including an enormous picture in a golden frame of a naked lady playing golf. Being a villain he liked pictures of naked ladies, but on the other hand he hated golf and all other wholesome sports, so even the picture was spoiled for him — he would have enjoyed a picture of a naked lady cheating at cards a great deal more. In fact his first words were words of complaint directed at the Nadger who stood among all this loot watching him out of astonished felt-penned eyes.

"I mean, stealing's one thing, and you've done well where the mere *amount* is concerned, I'll give you that," grumbled Jasper, "but why steal this particular stuff? Why seven dozen eggs? Why all this timber stain and why all this pet food? I'll tell you what – no more peccadillos for you! You can eat pet food from now on until it's all used up."

The Nadger gave a truly alarming growl and picked up a sharp cleaver that Jasper had not noticed until that moment. Jasper hastily grabbed the TV dinners and some shoe polish. If it came to a fight at least he would be able to throw something. However, a TV dinner (even one made with fish) did not seem much of a defence against a cleaver and he was looking around rather anxiously, while the Nadger growled softly and chopped at the air, when there came a loud knock at the door. The Nadger immediately dropped the cleaver and stiffened so that he looked like some sort of battered slot-machine. Jasper was a little confused, his brain softened by peppermint creams and fizzy wine. He answered the door — a sad mistake as there was a policeman on the other side of it as well as a group of angry people, all looking accusingly at Jasper.

"I am here to make certain inquiries," said the policeman, looking with astonishment at Jasper. It had to be admitted that a week of peppermint creams, bread and jam and fizzy wine had not improved him, and the fact that he was wearing crimson silk pyjamas with two buttons missing and clasping an armful of boot polish and TV fish dinners did not make a very good impression on the angry crowd.

"Are you the owner of a sort of tin man?" the policeman asked, taking out his notebook.

"Suppose I am — what about it?" asked Jasper crossly.

"I'll tell you what about it!" exclaimed a powerfully-built woman wearing a supermarket overall. "That wind-up Frankincense has visited my part of the supermarket and has stolen 106 pairs of stockings plus some frilly unmentionables."

"Nonsense madam," Jasper said crisply. "*If* (and I'm not admitting anything) *if*, I say, I did own a wind-up tin man and *if* he had visited your supermarket and stolen some stockings, I am sure he would only take about 102 pairs."

"Well, I'm sure he's the one that nicked my cleaver," cried an irate butcher.

"He's cleared the supermarket out of cat food," said a girl in a blue smock, "not to mention ball-point pens."

49

"Excuse me," said the policeman in a stern voice, silencing his supporters with severe frowns. Then turning to Jasper, he said, 'If you *was* the owner of said wind-up tin man. . . ."

"I admit nothing," Jasper interrupted haughtily.

". . . . I would like to come in and make an observation of your premises."

"I'd love to let you in," said Jasper with rapid and gushing enthusiasm. "Er — may I just run round the place with a duster? And there's a few things lying around. The dogs have just pulled the rubbish bag open. You know the way they do. If I can just have a moment to straighten things?"

"That will not be necessary," the policeman replied. "If I can just come in and look around. . . ."

"Do you have a warrant to search my house?" asked Jasper, crossing his fingers and dropping a fish dinner as he did so. The policeman looked a little anxious. "I couldn't think of letting you in without a warrant," Jasper went on. "You could be anyone. You could be a gang of ruffians dressed up as a policeman. I'll want to see your warrant."

The policeman laughed cheerily. "No need for that, sir. I assure you I am your genuine legal article."

"I am sure you are," Jasper said, "but I don't think we ought to go against the rules, do you?"

"Come on now, sir, let me in."

"No!" cried Jasper, and slammed and bolted the door. "Thank you!" he added through the keyhole. He heard a clatter of feet as the policeman, supported by angry shop-keepers, ran down the steps and out of the gate, no doubt to get a warrant to search the house.

"Now look what you've done!" Uncle Jasper cried, shaking a fish dinner at the Nadger. "Landed us right in it, haven't you? The idea is NOT to be caught, you know."

Jasper had planned to leave without paying the rent but not until he owed an extra month. Now he was forced to move very quickly, with no transport organized, no disguises, and only a few minutes to arrange things. But he was not a villain for nothing. Quick as a wink he had made wigs out of the floppy red mops, taken off his red pyjamas and put on blue jeans and a yellow T-shirt. For a moment he seriously thought of staining himself mahogany brown with the timber stain, but remembered the shoe polish in time. He emptied his life-savings into a bag made from his bed quilt and put it into a wheelbarrow, covering it over with a few dried-out peccadillos he found in the kitchen. Then he telephoned for a taxi.

A few minutes later two strange figures left the house. They passed the policeman on the road, warrant in hand, but he and his followers were so anxious to get into the house that they scarcely noticed the two red-headed, well-tanned strangers hurrying in the opposite direction.

As Jasper pushed his barrow of life-savings into the boot of the taxi he looked back at his old home with regret. Suddenly he realized that, when his seven sons came back, they wouldn't know where to find him. He had no address that he could leave. He didn't know where he was going to be himself. As he stood angry and helpless, pondering this for a moment, he was dimly aware of a bright poster which someone had glued on to a brick wall across the road:

TELEVISION REPAIR AND FORTUNE-TELLING SERVICE

It sounded rather fun. It sounded straightforward.

"Perhaps there is something to be said for an honest job," Jasper thought suddenly. It was a thought that occurred to him now and then when he saw trouble ahead.

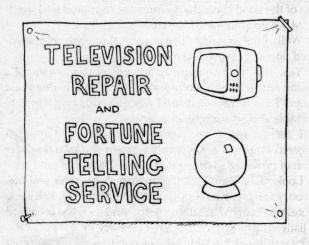

6

At the Tumble Inn Tavern

Some months later a dishevelled, haggard figure wearing an enormous moustache and a hunted look to match, burst from a wild stormy night into the cosy atmosphere of the Tumble Inn, a neighbourhood tavern in a cultured part of town.

"A glass of fizzy lemonade, please," he gasped desperately. The barman who had been mixing a particularly lurid drink and glancing morosely at a blank television screen, turned round and then glared at the newcomer, showing none of the good cheer that barmen are supposed to show.

"Make up your mind!" he ~ ~led.

"Well, I *did* say fizzy lemonade!" the newcomer stammered, looking furtive and terrified.

"Yes, and not two minutes ago you said you wanted a Flaming Arrow, a very sinful sort of drink," the barman said sourly. "I'm just mixing it and I was going to bring it over to your table and set it alight for you."

"I assure you," said the terrified one, "I have just staggered into your hostelry this moment and I would never dream of ordering anything that you could set fire to."

"Look mate," growled the barman, "you can't fool me. It's you, even if you have put on a false moustache. You came in here, you ordered a Flaming Arrow and then you collapsed in a listless fashion over. . . . oh, I *am* sorry sir."

For, sitting at the table he was pointing to, was another man collapsed in a listless fashion, who was the exact double of the first one, except that he was rather more furtive, possibly more terrified and certainly clean-shaven.

"Hello Julian," said this second man in a weary voice.

"Have you come to save me from myself?"

"Hello Jasper," said Julian, "actually I'm the one who needs saving." He sat down beside Jasper and the two brothers looked at each other.

"Never did I think to see you in a tavern, Julian!" said Jasper with a ghastly attempt at a smile. "Never did I think to

see you sporting a black moustache! You may possibly notice that I've been forced to shave mine off. May I ask why you've grown one?"

"Jasper," groaned Julian, "I'm being pursued by a Fiend Incarnate."

"Julian," cried Jasper, "so am I!"

They stared at each other wildly.

"You don't suppose it could be the same one, do you?" Julian breathed. "You wouldn't think there could be two Fiends Incarnate in the same city at the same time. Has yours got golden hair, blue eyes and a clean apron?"

"Great Scruffling Tomwoggles! No!" Jasper laughed bitterly. "Is yours made of tins and wire with a frying-pan for a face?"

"Dear me no — not in the slightest." Julian looked perplexed.

"There you are then. It can't be the same one. Two Fiends Incarnate are getting around simultaneously." Jasper sank lower in his seat. "They're obviously quite different ones."

"I suppose they come in all shapes and sizes," Julian sighed, "and mine spends so much time with me that it wouldn't have time to pursue you too. I liked mine to begin with, mind you."

"And I liked mine," cried Jasper. "I thought he was really promising."

"Yours was a boy then?" asked Julian delicately. "Mine was female."

"I don't really know what mine was — is —" Jasper mumbled disconsolately. "It could have been anything or nothing."

The barman now came forward with two drinks — one was tall and cold, frosted with ice and sugar, clinking musically with ice-blocks. The other was shorter and fiercer, composed of three beautifully-coloured liqueurs and burning with a lovely blue flame.

"I'm sorry if I was a bit terse with you gents a moment back," the barman said in a very oily voice. "I thought you was having me on, likewise I'm a bit of a prey to melancholy at present because the TV's broken down and I'm missing me programmes."

"Indeed!" said Jasper with withering sarcasm, but the barman wanted to talk about his broken television set and would not be put off.

"I've sent for the experts," he went on, "and they've promised to send none other than Mr. Laculagi all the way from the establishment. Everyone's talking about them and how reliable they are with TVs and stereos and pocket calculators and electric typewriters and so on. It takes Mr. Laculagi but a second or two to restore the old goggle box to its former functionings, and people say he normally fixes them better than when they was new. There's people deliberately sabotaging their TVs just so they can get Mr. Laculagi to come round and mend them."

"Tchaaa!" exclaimed the impatient Jasper, making a sort of wet, clicking sound used by villains from time to time. Julian gave him a reproving look, and said to the man in kind tones, "Who are these experts you have summoned, may I ask?"

"I keep telling you! Them!" said the barman and pointed to a poster on the wall.

"It's very bright!" said Julian rather critically. "Ah yes. . . . Television Repair, Fortune-Telling and Suburban Transport Service with Associated Gourmet Parrot Restaurant, Market Garden and Parrot Reference Library. I've seen these posters everywhere lately."

"Their bus goes by here every night now," the barman said, "taking hoards of ravenous diners out to the restaurant. The vegetables is fresher than fresh. You can pick your own cabbage and have it cooked up before your very eyes. Of course the meals are fabulously expensive, but people are saving up and getting there somehow."

"Very gratifying for the proprietors," said Julian wistfully.

"Not only that," the barman went on, warming to his subject. "Those that are rich enough and brave enough get their fortunes told. And the bookish ones can check up on obscure facts, historical riddles and problematical mysteries and enigmas between the main course and the afters. The librarian is always on hand with his team of trained parrots."

"They must be making a packet!" said Jasper sourly. "You know, Julian, the last few weeks have made me lose faith in my own chosen profession, I don't mind telling you. All my life-savings gone, used up in rapid escapes by taxi, or else abandoned along the way, and my seven boys vanished. . . . !"

"Your sons? Gone? All of them?" cried Julian. "How terrible! My little Prudence has vanished too. The police have utterly failed to locate her."

"Hardly surprising! They've spent all their time chasing me," said Jasper gloomily.

"It was that doll you sent her — that Lilly Rose Blossom — that Fiend Incarnate. . . ."

"Hang on a moment!" Jasper sat up. "Lilly Rose Blossom wasn't a Fiend Incarnate. She was only a sickly simpering walkie-talkie doll that Genghis had put too much of something into. If you want to talk about Fiends Incarnate, what about the Nadger, eh? What about that? If you knew the time I've had, moving house every few days, every few *hours* sometimes, hounded by the police, and angry supermarket managers and check-out girls. He's got the idea of stealing all right, but he's fascinated by supermarkets. He doesn't sleep and he doesn't stop and his idea is to bring everything he steals to me. Imagine waking up in the morning surrounded by packets of frozen pastry, paper towels, icing sugar, gingernuts, lavatory paper and nutmeg graters. He's got no judgement — no judgement at all — furniture polish and sardines, fly killer, hair shampoo — it's all one to him. I've had to escape from a hundred places, and sometimes I haven't even had time to get behind with the rent. The Nadger's chasing me with his arms full of cooking foil and fish fingers, and the police are chasing both of us, confound them."

"They're only doing their duty, Jasper," said Julian.

"Don't give me that! Their duty is to be out catching the REAL criminals, or finding your little Prudence, not hounding a worried man who's lost all his life-savings and is worrying about his seven lost sons. Oh, but you don't know what it is to suffer!"

"Oh don't I?" cried Julian, roused to an un-Julian-like fury at last. "Well, you don't know what it's like being kept awake until all hours of the night listening to seven hundred and thirty-four Improving Tales by Nanny Gringe. You don't know what it's like to be drenched in sugar and drowned in golden syrup, to have the very paragons taken out of your soup and to be forced to live on distilled water. You don't know what it's like to have a golden-haired doll following you wherever you go, urging you to improve your life, crying over you in public places like the bus and the bank and the Post Office, urging you to give up your sinful ways. . . . And truly Jasper, I have my faults, but I can't think of a single sinful way that I can give up. I don't smoke. I don't drink intoxicating drinks. I'm a vegetarian and I behave in a kindly fashion to all. So when Lilly Rose Blossom urges me to give up my sinful ways and reads me improving stories until four o'clock in the morning — well, what I say is, that isn't Lilly Rose Blossom, that's a Fiend Incarnate."

"Rightly said, brother," exclaimed Jasper and the twins clasped hands in true brotherhood for the first time in many, many years.

As this moving scene took place a tall figure entered the Tumble Inn, bringing with him a large canvas tool-kit, with roller-skates riveted to the bottom of it so that it could be wheeled along beside its owner. What could be seen of the man looked young but much of his face was hidden by a large chestnut-coloured moustache, as large as the one Jasper had shaved off and a lot larger than the one Julian had grown. The barman hurried forward in an obsequious fashion.

"Mr. Laculagi?" he cried. "Oh I *am* glad to see you, Mr. Laculagi. My TV has been on the blink for nearly two hours and they have been two hours of horror and desolation for me."

"There! There! All will be well now," said Mr. Laculagi, patting his arm in a reassuring fashion and speaking in a deep, resonant voice that inspired calm confidence. "We — that is — I have never failed with a TV yet. We will restore it to you full of pep, with clean, fresh breath and hair on its chest." At this moment Mr. Laculagi's eyes fell on Jasper and Julian and he stood like one who suddenly recognizes a long-lost relative.

"They're just customers — nobodies — don't worry about them," said the barman, fawning. "Take no notice of *them*,

Mr. Laculagi. Look, the TV is over here, Mr. Laculagi. . . . Laculagi, what an intellectual name."

"Italian!" said Mr. Laculagi absent-mindedly. He seemed fascinated by Jasper and Julian who shrank under his gaze and tried to hide their faces behind their drinks.

"I need to commune with the television set," Mr. Laculagi said at last. "I need to meditate, to identify with its interests. Is there anywhere we can be alone together?"

"I'll push it into the next room," said the barman, eagerly. "No one will disturb you in there." And he and Mr. Laculagi tenderly guided the television set into the next room, while Jasper and Julian watched curiously.

"I thought that the tool-bag seemed to wriggle a bit," said Julian doubtfully. "It looked as if it had something alive in it."

"Never mind the tool-bag," Jasper exclaimed. "Rumbling Gradgenappits! Why did he look at us like that? And he reminds me of someone, you know. I swear I've seen him somewhere before. The rest of his face doesn't go with that moustache, but I can't be sure whether it's the face or the moustache I remember. I do know that they weren't together when I last saw them." He shook his head. "But I mustn't get led astray by inessentials. Now we are together what can we do to escape our unwelcome companions? I'm sure the Nadger is not too far away. He has followed me everywhere until now."

"Lilly Rose Blossom has always managed to find me in a very short time," admitted Julian, "though she may not come into a tavern, of course."

The barman reappeared from the other room. "What a lovely fellow," he declared, beaming. "He's promised me he'll have the television fixed in a few minutes by a special process that never works when anyone else is in the room."

"My Prudence was a whizz with television sets," Julian recalled. "But Lilly Rose Blossom won't even let me turn our set on now."

61

At this moment, faintly but none the less clearly, there came the sound of breaking glass and screaming. The brothers stiffened with apprehension. The barman ran to the tavern door.

"What's going on?" he cried. "What a scene! Some nut is trying to make off with an armful of soap powder from the supermarket. Gor! Look! There are police all over him. He's thrown them off as if they were thistledown. Oh dear! There goes the soap powder into a puddle — what a mess." He looked back at Jasper and Julian. "He's a really weird-looking guy. You won't believe this, but he looks as if he's got a frying-pan for a head."

Jasper half rose from his seat.

"Still, he ought to be stopped," the barman said. "It's upsetting the passers-by. There's a little kid there and she looks very upset. A dear little girl with lovely golden curls in a blue dress."

Julian half rose from his seat too.

"The soap powder's foaming up like no one's business," the barman said. "It's spreading down the street. The cops might lose him after all."

With a bound Jasper was across the room, shaking the man's arm urgently.

"Listen!" he hissed. "We've got to leave. We must go now. We've got to get out straightaway."

"So?" the barman said blankly. "Feel free to walk out any time you like."

"We need disguises. We're being followed by enemies," Jasper explained. "What can you give us to help us disguise ourselves?"

The barman looked at them. "Towels!" he said at last. "Towels! But it'll cost you."

"We'll take them," Jasper cried. "Come on, Julian. I've still got some brown boot polish. Honestly, this last week I seem to have spent hours either putting polish on or taking it off."

"It seems so useless," said Julian, "I think I'll just give in."

"Never!" shouted Jasper. "Show a bold front! No surrender! Look on the bright side! Never say die! Nil desperandum! While there's life there's hope!"

"You have convinced me," Julian said, and the brothers vanished into the men's washroom with an armful of towels.

Mr. Laculagi, clutching his tool-bag, suddenly emerged from the room next door, pushing the television set in front of him. It was working again, showing a picture of crystal clarity and wonderfully rich colour. The barman paid Mr. Laculagi with folding money and many flowery compliments, showed him to a door into a side street and then went back to the front door to see what was happening with the soapsuds, the policeman and the supermarket thief.

The door of the men's washroom opened and Jasper and Julian appeared, transformed by boot polish and towels into Eastern gentlemen, their brown faces wearing inscrutable expressions of oriental calm. But the barman was too interested in what was going on down the street to notice them.

"Someone's coming out of the soapsuds!" he shouted. "Someone's getting free. Oh deary me! It's that there supermarket pilferer with the head like a frying-pan. The little girl in blue is close behind him. They're coming this way. Wouldn't be surprised if they was planning to come in here."

"Don't let him in. He's a thief and a vagabond!" shouted Jasper.

"Don't let her in. She's under age for being allowed in taverns," yelled Julian.

"I can't stop them if they're determined, can I?" answered the barman nervously. "That tin chap looks nasty. There's only me here, isn't there?"

"You poltroon!" snarled Jasper. "Is there another way out of this cursed tavern?"

"Sure!" said the barman, still gazing down the street with great interest. "Straight through there to the bus-stop, the way Mr. Laculagi went."

Jasper and Julian scrambled out of the side door just as a bright blue bus painted with yellow suns, orange stars and pink parrots pulled up at the bus-stop. Mr. Laculagi climbed on first, with Jasper and Julian fretting at his heels. The bus driver looked at them in astonishment. He seemed very young for a bus driver but he must have been of a reasonable age for he had a large golden moustache, about the same size as Mr. Laculagi's.

As they collapsed on to the front seat, the bus drew away down the road. Glancing back, Julian saw through the windows of the Tumble Inn Tavern the Nadger bowl the barman over and stand on him, while Lilly Rose Blossom smiled her candy-floss smile — a smile that now seemed terrible to him.

"Look," Julian whispered, but Jasper was frowning to himself.

"I have the strangest feeling that I know that bus driver," he muttered. "Either I know him or I know his moustache — one or the other and I can't remember which."

"That's the trouble with a fugitive's life," sighed Julian. "After a while you think you know everyone or that everyone knows you. It's all illusion really."

Across the aisle, in the other pair of front seats, sat Mr. Laculagi watching them out of the corner of his eye. The back of the bus driver's neck seemed very familiar to Jasper. He slumped back in his seat, frowning to himself, then he sat up again.

"By the way," he asked, "where are we going? What bus is this, and where is it off to?"

"We're on our way to the much praised Parrot Restaurant," Mr. Laculagi told him. "Don't worry about a thing! Relax and enjoy the journey. The Parrot Restaurant is the place where everyone on the bus is longing to go. You'll love it when you get there."

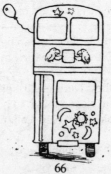

7

A Colourful Bus Ride to the Parrot Restaurant

When they dared to look around at last, Julian and Jasper were surprised and even alarmed.

The bus was a beautiful pink inside with purple parrots painted all over the ceiling. All the seats were full of passengers carrying pink balloons with purple parrots printed on them. There was a scent of flowers, and the music of harps and xylophones filled the air. Neither Jasper nor Julian could remember this sort of thing on any bus they had travelled on before.

They both had the distinct feeling of being watched. Julian looked up and, in the mirror over the driving seat, met the eyes of the bus driver. Jasper looked left and found Mr. Laculagi glancing at him yet again. They both pretended not to notice and started talking to each other.

"You do miss the boys, I suppose, now they've gone?" Julian asked Jasper quietly.

"Miss them?" Jasper cried. "*Miss* them?" he repeated rather uneasily, for although there was a lot of noise in the bus he felt there were ears all around him especially listening to what he was saying. "I miss them *terribly*. Their very names ring in my memories like golden bells."

"As for me, I often dream of hearing my little Prudence's voice," sighed Julian.

At that moment they were electrified to hear a voice, strange and muffled but clear enough to be heard among the harps and laughter, asking, "Hey Caligula! Caligula! Why don't you let me out?"

"Did you hear *that*?" exclaimed Jasper. "The very name —

Caligula — in the air!''

"Did you hear that?" exclaimed Julian. "The very voice of Prudence! What did I tell you?"

"I must be haunted with remorse." Jasper shrugged his shoulders. "Well, I'm not surprised. I thought I was."

"Me too," said Julian.

"Excuse me!" said Mr. Laculagi, leaning across towards them and giving his tool-kit a fairly gentle push with his foot.

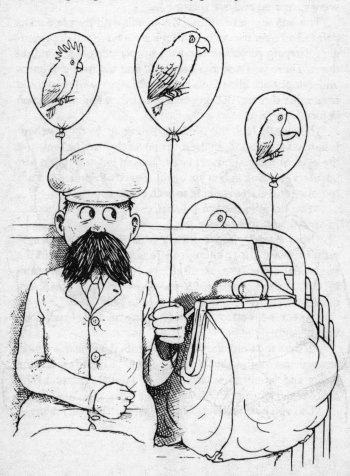

"I do hope you are all right. You seemed a little agitated back there, as if you were fleeing from some danger."

"Well, we're both being pursued by Fiends Incarnate," said Jasper, "both of us by a different one."

"Ah, that explains it," said Mr. Laculagi. "Well, if I were you I'd go all the way to the Parrot Restaurant. They're very select in a sort of liberal way, and I'm sure they wouldn't permit a Fiend Incarnate to cross their threshold."

"It's a good idea," Julian said thoughtfully. "And I'm hungry, too — but I am a vegetarian. I don't know if the Parrot Restaurant is quite the place for me."

"I'm not a vegetarian, but I don't fancy parrot," Jasper grumbled, looking doubtful.

"The parrots aren't there to be eaten," Mr. Laculagi reassured him. "I don't think they've ever served parrot. No, the parrots are part of the Reference Library Service."

"I thought libraries were concerned with reading and books," said Julian with suspicion.

"Oh well, there are plenty of books, too. . . . books, documents, filmstrips, posters and original manuscripts," Mr. Laculagi told him. "Going into parrots is just another library extension. In fact, this library is really pioneering a new service. For instance, if you are interested in, say, *Alice in Wonderland* or in stamp collecting or in the history of Upper Mongolia, you simply ask for the appropriate parrot, mentioning the language you prefer, and the parrot will be brought to your table to entertain you with conversation about your hobby during your meal."

"It sounds expensive," Jasper said, with a melancholy smile.

"Do try it," advised Mr. Laculagi, "I think you'll find that, in your case, in your two cases that is, they will feed you entirely free of charge. And I don't expect you'd be charged for the fortune-teller, or the parrot, should you require one."

"Do they have a parrot that talks about Safe-cracking and Bank Robbery?" asked Jasper with a faint smile.

"Yes, but only in Spanish," said Mr. Laculagi reprovingly.

"Let me get this straight," Julian frowned. "You mean that they will give us a free meal, and — and these other services you describe?"

"Exactly so." Mr. Laculagi nodded.

"But why should they?" asked Julian, frowning still. "I mean — well — why should they?"

70

"The proprietors believe that twins will bring them good luck and so they're always very generous to twins. They encourage them to come as often as possible." They had stopped at the traffic lights and it was Jasper's turn to look up into the mirror above the windscreen that enabled the driver to see what was going on in his bus.

He met the gaze of the driver who was watching them closely once more, though pretending he was merely checking up on the rest of his high-spirited bus-load of passengers.

At that very moment a short figure in a pink and purple uniform came down the aisle of the bus — a mere boy one would have said, had it not been for his large red moustache. In fact he looked very like the bus driver, if you chose to overlook the colour of their moustaches.

"You gentlemen are to travel free," he said in a high-pitched voice. "This ride is on the house."

"I thought it was on the bus," Jasper muttered, causing the conductor to look at him rather sternly.

71

"Two balloons for you gentlemen. One each!" the boy said, giving them each a pink balloon with a purple parrot on it. "The Parrot Restaurant hopes you will accept these with our compliments."

"Very nice!" exclaimed Julian with delight. "I say — the Parrot Restaurant certainly knows how to make people feel wanted."

But Jasper accepted his balloon with suspicion. His old villain's training made it hard for him to sit holding a balloon; he was also teased and tantalized by the resemblance that the bus driver, the conductor and Mr. Laculagi had to one another, and to some person or persons he knew he had met some time in the past and could almost, but not quite, remember.

Or was it their moustaches he remembered? Jasper was not sure.

8

The Parrot Restaurant

Clutching their balloons, Jasper and Julian scrambled out of the bus and into the foyer of the Parrot Restaurant.

Here, in the rose pink glow, the crowd from the bus was met by a mysterious figure wearing a silver mask, and holding a large glass bubble that shone with rainbow-coloured lights.

"I am the fortune-teller," said this apparition, "and I foretell that you will all have a magnificent dinner with entertainment of a totally unexpected kind. Personal fortunes will be told at your table later in the evening, should you require them."

"What sort of a restaurant is this?" asked Jasper pettishly. "Where has Mr. Laculagi gone?"

But within the next few minutes he forgot about the nebulous television repair man for they were shown to the best table in the restaurant by a very smooth, though very short, waiter and given an enormous menu.

"For you, gentlemen, the food is entirely free," said the waiter, his voice squeaky behind a large black moustache.

"There's another one of them," said Jasper nervously. "Do you suppose they come in a set?" But Julian, glancing down the menu, was turning pale with shock. It was so rich and varied that even reading it proved almost too much for a man used to the blandness of paragon soup and the milk of human kindness. A second waiter, a short one with a ginger moustache and a ginger beard held on by rubber bands around the ears, brought a wine list.

Jasper stared at him sharply. "Weren't you — aren't you

the bus conductor?" he asked.

"I can be — I have been — I will be again," was the strange answer. "But my main work is gardening. Choose which wine you most fancy. It is all on the house, you know." And off he went.

A moment later, a third waiter appeared — the smallest one so far. Bowing low, he presented a third card, beautifully decorated with paintings of birds, butterflies and leaves and headed 'Parrot List'.

"Parrot list?" Julian exclaimed and turned to question the waiter still further, but he was already gliding away, and when they looked they saw that he had added to his height by wearing roller-skates. He wove in and out of the tables with incredible skill, distributing Parrot Lists to the delighted clientele.

"Well, I've dined in some funny places in my time," Jasper said explosively, " but I've never seen anything to equal this."

But Julian looked around like one enchanted. At the end of the big room the chef could be seen working at a beautiful bench of pink marble. Fruit trees in tubs stood around the walls and many garden boxes filled with wonderfully green vegetables which were picked and cooked while you waited.

75

As the smallest waiter skated by, Jasper whispered, "I'll tell you something else, Julian. I don't think that waiter is more than about nine or ten, and yet he has a fluffy grey moustache."

"Shhh! The librarian is going to sing," Julian answered.

A sudden shaft of golden light fell in the centre of the room and into its bright circle stepped the librarian, a dazzling figure in golden tights, wearing a golden mask, with gold-rimmed spectacles put on over it. One of the waiters struck up a jolly tune on a mouth-organ and the golden librarian began his song:

When you sit down to dine, while selecting the wine
And deciding on cabbage or carrot,
Pray don't feel resigned to neglecting your mind —
Choose a fluent and well-informed parrot.

Our parrots are firm in their knowledge of German,
French, Russian, Norwegian or Spanish.
In Greek or in Dutch their philosophy's such
That your doubts and dissensions will vanish.

Cockatoos and macaws will expound without pause
On topics that tease at your mind.
Astrophysics, black holes, common markets, jam rolls,
In a manner relaxed and refined.

There is *so* much to learn! Oh, which way can you turn
For the knowledge that study can bring?
Give a parrot a trial and you'll soon start to smile
When you find it exactly the thing.

There was enthusiastic applause following this scholarly song.

"That's not like any librarian I've ever met," said Julian, a touch disapprovingly.

"A *lot* of things are funny here. I keep telling you that," muttered Jasper, watching waiters gliding past.

When it came to ordering dinner, Julian, rather as a matter of duty, asked for paragons, and Jasper inquired for peccadillos, but these were not obtainable and the normally courteous waiter sneered at the inquiry in a distinctly savage way.

"You must try something new," he said. "Why dine out in order to have the same things that you have at home?"

So Jasper had a delicious onion soup followed by eels in green sauce, followed by loin fillets of pork with prunes and

cream sauce, and Julian had watercress soup, an avocado pear with lemon juice, and a mixed vegetable dish including grilled mushrooms, asparagus and braised red cabbage in red wine and chestnuts. These exotic delicacies were washed down with pink champagne. A rare hyacinthine macaw was wheeled over to their table and recited the poems from *Alice in Wonderland* in several different languages. It was a most delightful and cultural occasion.

"Who would have thought it?" said Julian wonderingly. "One moment fleeing from Lilly Rose Blossom and the Nadger, the next dining in undreamed-of luxury."

"Here's a toast," said Jasper, "to us, to the dark and the light that keep the balance of the world between them."

"A charming toast!" said a voice.

Jasper looked up. The fortune-teller stood beside him, beautiful and ominous in his silver mask.

"I don't want my fortune told," growled Jasper hastily.

"A pity!" said the fortune-teller, in a faintly mocking voice. "You are such good subjects, being twins. Are you still devoted to heroism, Julian? Has villainy grown boring yet, Jasper?"

The brothers stared at him with the alarm often shown by those whose secrets are laid bare. "You have fled through the night to the haven of the Parrot Restaurant," the fortune-teller went on, "but trouble follows hard on your heels. You have evaded your pursuing demons — but not lost them."

"I don't want to hear any more," said Jasper. "I was enjoying myself a few minutes ago."

"Aren't you interested — just a tiny bit curious — to know when doom is going to strike?" asked the fortune-teller.

Jasper and Julian looked at each other in a quavering way. Then they looked at the fortune-teller.

"O.K. wise guy!" Jasper almost snarled, in the old villainous way. "When is doom going to strike, if you're so clever?"

"It's going to strike. . . ." the fortune-teller looked over their heads as if consulting an unseen clock that hung in mid-air. "It's going to strike NOW." As he spoke the restaurant door burst open and a rattling, clanking sound announced the entrance of the Nadger.

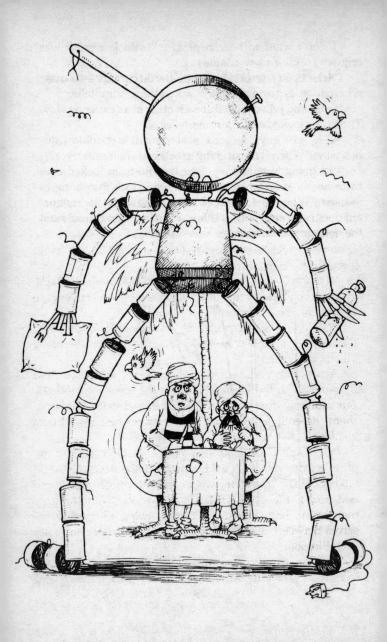

9

No Escape from the Fiends Incarnate

He stood at the door of the Parrot Restaurant with his arms full of stolen supplies of self-raising flour, imitation strawberry essence and dish-washing liquid. He had never looked more threatening than he did in the ghostly pink light. Beside him, absolutely spotless even at the end of a scrambling, searching day, was Lilly Rose Blossom, all golden curls, fluttering eyelashes and candy-floss smile. Julian and Jasper stared at the two creatures in horror.

"They're monsters," breathed Julian, "both of them. How could I have ever wanted my lovely brown Prudence to be like Lilly Rose Blossom?"

"Galloping Grudgenugglers!" swore Jasper. "How could I have ever remotely wanted my seven boys to be really villainous villains?"

Across the polished floor the Nadger and Lilly Rose Blossom advanced implacably upon the cowering brothers. But suddenly the fortune-teller moved and stood in front of them, defending Julian and Jasper from their unwelcome shadows.

"Go back! Go back!" their parrot shouted, and all the other parrots danced a wild dance and shouted, "Go back! Go back!" The small wine waiter with the ginger moustache and beard, the even smaller parrot waiter with the grey moustache, both joined the fortune-teller, ranging themselves between Jasper and Julian and the Nadger and Lilly Rose Blossom.

"It is my duty to save Uncle Julian from his own imperfections," said Lilly Rose Blossom, all golden syrup and tempered steel. "I am going to take him home and read improving tales to him. I am sure there is hope for him."

The head waiter with the black moustache and the chef came and stood with the first two waiters and the fortune-teller.

"I've got this armful of stuff for the boss," croaked the Nadger. "He's got to find us somewhere to live and cook me some shenanigans."

The mere mention of shenanigans caused a tremor to pass over Jasper's face. He had quite gone off them himself.

The librarian in his golden mask and tights joined the waiter, the fortune-teller and the chef.

"You can't keep them from us," said Lilly Rose Blossom. "We know our duty and we are tireless. We aren't mere flesh and blood. We are creatures of science and enchantment."

People in the restaurant were listening full of interest, thinking this must be a shadow show put on for their special benefit.

"We have the right!" the Nadger grated. "They *gave* us the right. They welcomed us. Jasper and I, we've shared shenanigans and pared peccadillos together."

"I've supped dear Uncle Julian's paragon soup with him," simpered Lilly Rose Blossom.

"But so have we!" said a new voice — a resonant voice, a voice of power. "Before you came on the scene Jasper often served us Hooligan Pie and we ate it together."

It was none other than Mr. Laculagi skating his TV repair bag over the restaurant floor. Inside it something stirred and unfolded. Out of the bag rose a thin, brown, smiling girl with a smudge of oil on one cheek and a screwdriver in her hand. "And I've eaten many a paragon with Julian," she cried.

"Lilly Rose Blossom, you are just an invention of ours," said Mr. Laculagi. "A wicked whim! A caprice!" He removed his chestnut moustache.

"Caligula!" yelled Jasper and then was silent, staring in

82

amazement. The chef removed his moustache, the waiters removed theirs, the librarian and the fortune-teller took off their masks – and there stood Nero, Belshazzar, Adolph and little Jack! There stood Genghis and Tarquin revealed to all.

"Mr. Nadger, you are nothing but a pile of tins, wires and bottle-tops," said the girl in the tool-bag. "I know all your secrets and circuits, for I put them together."

"It's my Prudence!" Julian cried.

The Nadger and Lilly Rose Blossom edged away from the line of children towards Jasper and Julian.

"You cannot turn us from our prey," said the Nadger. "They made us too simple in the wrong way. We are their true children, the children of their ideas. You are nothing but blood and bones, but we are their thoughts. You grow tired but we go on and on for ever, unchanging."

The Nadger and Lilly Rose Blossom dodged as Adolph and Jack skated out to meet them. They dodged as golden Genghis and black Tarquin moved on them like matadors.

"Are you going to stand for ever between us and them?" asked the Nadger in a scornful, creaking voice. "Watch as you will, we will get them sooner or later."

"If we don't destroy you first!" called Prudence. She advanced on the Nadger, her faithful soldering iron in her hand. "One false move from you, and your sprockets will be melted down on to your transistors."

The Nadger could not turn pale but at the sight of the soldering iron he gave a great clanking shudder. Anyone could see he was highly alarmed.

"Are you planning to melt me down too?" asked Lilly Rose Blossom sweetly and there was a stir of anxiety. It is one thing to melt down a Nadger's sprockets, but another thing to melt a robot that looks like a little girl in a frilly apron.

"It is true," said Lilly Rose Blossom, "that the Nadger has stolen a wide variety of goods from supermarkets — but is it not because that is what he was MADE to do? It is true he is a collection of tins wired together, but by now he has a name and he knows himself. Is it fair to destroy him simply for being what he was invented to be?

"Was he invented with kindly intentions?" Lilly Rose Blossom went on. "Was I? We are blamed for our too-muchness and our too-littleness, but we were animated for your purposes and now your purpose is to destroy us, to punish *us* for *your* success. Is it my fault that the imperfections of those around me force me to try to improve my companions?" She looked at Caligula with her candy-floss smile and Caligula blushed and scratched his head.

"You can stop playing the game of villains and heroes when you want to," Lilly Rose Blossom continued. "You can become actors, chefs, gardeners, librarians, fortune-tellers, bus drivers, painters, electronic engineers and waiters. The Nadger and I are bound, by wrong measurements and by wickedness circuits, to be heroine and villain for ever. You can enjoy eels in tarragon sauce and grilled mushrooms, but we are bound to eat paragons and peccadillos all our days."

Julian rose sadly to his feet. "Lilly Rose Blossom is right," he said. "I owe her a lot for she has enabled me to recognize my own too-muchness in certain directions. I don't want to lose Lilly Rose Blossom. If I have to listen to Nanny Gringe's improving tales for the rest of her days, well, I have to, and that's that. It may be I shall improve along lines that Nanny Gringe could never imagine."

"Curse it!" cried Jasper. "Sprongling Cagglewidgets! A true villain wouldn't hesitate to get rid of the Nadger. He's been a real embarrassment to me. What's gone wrong with my Villainy? Do I have to put up with him whiffling around, filling wherever I'm staying with quick frozen peas and soap powder? It seems I do!"

Then, for the second time that evening, the door of the Parrot Restaurant burst open. In came fifteen policemen, some of them still covered in soapsuds. They were led by a Detective Inspector — and none other than the one who had been so affected by Caligula's acting at the select School for Villains.

The Detective Inspector's blue official gaze fell on Jasper. "Ah sir," he said briskly, "is it you that superintends the activities of that well-known supermarket thief, the Nadger?"

"I take no responsibility," said Jasper quickly.

"Because, sir, I have a proposal that it would be to his advantage to listen to," said the Detective Inspector. "I am empowered to offer him a lucrative job where his talents will be appreciated. We have this police college, you see," he went on, "and our young men are supposed to get practice dealing with various crimes; it might be Car Conversion or Widow and Orphan Grinding or even Assault and Battery.

Well, we have a simulated supermarket there done up just like a real one, with Specials and soap powder and those little trolleys. . . . The Nadger can come there and steal to his heart's content, morning, noon and night, and your young hopefuls can get a bit of practice at dealing with a supermarket thief. I am authorized to offer him a nice room with a view and with his dinner provided."

"Peccadillos?" asked Caligula.

"Peccadillos, armadillos — whatever he fancies, we can arrange a bit of," said the Detective Inspector firmly.

The Nadger turned his astonished frying-pan face to look at Jasper.

"You — you go!" said Jasper. "Don't mind me, old fellow. Don't let me stand in your way. This is a great chance for you — a chance for unlimited Villainy without harassment by the police."

"Ahem!" said Lilly Rose Blossom, looking sternly at the Nadger. "I shall go with him, for I can see that improving him will be a real challenge, he is so very far sunk in iniquity. May I take this valuable book, Uncle Julian? After all, you have heard nearly all of it, and I am sure you would not let the lust for material possessions stand in the way of another creature's redemption."

"No — of course I wouldn't. Please do take it," murmured Julian, shuddering at the sight of Nanny Gringe's *One Thousand Improving Tales* in its brown and gold binding. "Accept it with my thanks and affection. It could not be sacrificed to a nobler cause."

Prudence smiled. She had unscrewed the Nadger's back plate and was just checking up on his interior wiring and transistors. She adjusted the gauge in his back so that it would read VILLAINOUS and not SUPERVILLAINOUS and quickly, with the skill of inspiration, incorporated an improvement circuit. She wasn't quite sure how this would work, and there was not time to run tests, but she thought that continued

87

listening to improving stories might modify the Nadger so that he would improve to the point of being merely BAD—or even DOWNRIGHT INCONSIDERATE. At least he would enjoy listening to the improving stories as much as Lilly Rose Blossom enjoyed reading them.

"Ready?" asked the Detective Inspector as Prudence screwed up the Nadger's back plate again.

"He's fine! He's ready to take up his new duties," said Prudence.

The Nadger must have been in a good mood, for he went fairly quietly, simply breaking a chair with a single blow as he left and clanking a bit in his tinny, rattling way.

Jasper gave a huge sigh of relief and beamed all over his face, and though Julian was trying to look grave and regretful he couldn't keep it up and he sighed and beamed too.

So Jasper was reunited with his seven sons, and Julian with his single tall, brown, tangled daughter, screwdriver and all.

10

Plans and Prophesies

By two o'clock in the morning all the patrons of the Parrot Restaurant had gone home full of delicious food and richly entertained, vowing to start saving at once to come back again. The two happy families, Jasper and his seven sons, Julian and his only daughter, were left alone together to count the enormous profits made from yet another successful evening. All around them cockatoos and macaws watched with sympathetic interest.

"You know," said Jasper as Prudence counted the money, "I think I'll retire from Villainy."

"And I'll retire from the Saintly Life," Julian added.

"I do so without regret," said Jasper. "There's always plenty of young blood coming on in my profession. The future of Villainy is in safe hands."

"I'm not too sure about Saintliness," said Julian doubtfully, looking suddenly concerned. "Perhaps I shouldn't desert my post."

"Oh Dad," said Prudence, "there's a higher rate of Lofty Sentiment and Bitter Remorse now than ever before in history."

"But what about Self-Denial?" asked Julian, and Prudence was silent.

"Well, more people are becoming vegetarians, I can tell you that," Nero declared. "There's a constant demand for Celery Victor, mushrooms and onions in sour cream and potato pancakes with apple sauce, not to mention avocado and tomato cocktails."

"I'm having to plant more cucumbers for pickles,"

89

Belshazzar pointed out. Julian let himself be convinced.

"You see, we need you here," Adolph assured him. "Caligula has got a part in a big play in the city and when rehearsals start he's not going to be able to be Mr. Laculagi any more. Mr. Laculagi will have to retire, but we'll still need someone to take Prudence around in the tool-kit, and who better than her own father, eh? And in the evening you can be a waiter if you like."

"I'll take on the job of treasurer," offered Jasper. "I've had a lot of experience with money."

"No, Father!" said Caligula, looking at him sternly. "You might be tempted out of retirement and try to start off another lot of life-savings. . . . No, you would be the ideal man to take over responsibility for our expanding parrot empire. You had a year or two of Piracy in your youth and I feel that should give you a sympathetic parrot background."

"Great Whilloping Gradgenuzzlers!" swore Jasper. "What a superb idea!" The parrots all cackled and those with crests raised them approvingly.

"Great Whilloping Gradgenuzzlers!" they repeated.

"I don't know!" said Genghis doubtfully. "You know parrots learn to swear very easily, and these parrots have been specially trained to be a useful branch of our reference library."

"Oh, a few oaths will pep up the information no end," promised Jasper eagerly. "Instead of simply saying, for example, 'A laser is a device for directing common light in completely parallel lines without diffusion or dispersion' the parrot will say, 'Thundering Maledictions! I tell you a laser is a bindlespang device for directing common light in completely parallel lines without any grimtucketing diffusion or snufwinkling dispersion.' That'll bring the whole thing to life."

"I see what you mean," Genghis said. "You feel, Father, that a greater degree of verbal liberation and latitude will intensify the impact of the communication of any system of knowledge?"

"I couldn't have put it better myself," exclaimed Jasper. "In fact, I've often thought of making a sort of study — a scholarly study that is — of swearing. And now, with this team of parrots at my disposal, I shall give the project serious thought."

"Great Whilloping Gradgenuzzlers!" the parrots chorused.

"I may have to balance things out by studying exclamations of an emphatic but refined nature," said Julian quietly.

"Just think of all I'll have to fit on our next poster," sighed little Jack. "Television Repair, Fortune-telling and Suburban Transport Service with Associated Gourmet Parrot Restaurant, Market Garden, Parrot Reference Library and Exclamation and Expletive School. I'll need a lot more paint."

"We mustn't forget to check up on the Nadger and Lilly Rose Blossom from time to time," said Julian. "In a way they are the creations of all of us and we are responsible for their well-being."

"Clotzwinkle!" cried Jasper. "I've seen enough of that pair. Still you're right, though. I was very fond of that Nadger for a while. I don't want to lose touch with him entirely, confound his clattering old wickedness circuits."

Tarquin pulled on his silver mask and put his fortune-teller's globe on the floor in front of them even though it was shooting out rainbow-coloured sparks.

"I foretell. . . ." he intoned in his mysterious echoing fortune-teller's voice ". . . . I foretell a mixed-biscuit future for all of us."

"Happiness?" asked Julian.

"Some of that!" said Tarquin.

"Wealth?" suggested Jasper eagerly.

"Some of that too," Tarquin replied. "Some of what we want and some of what we don't expect. Something of what we plan, and a lot of surprises as well. Over the ocean of our intention sails the good ship Serendipity.

"Marvellous, isn't it?" Jasper said sarcastically. "Give a boy a bit of independence and he goes around spouting words his poor old father would never dare to employ. Put it in English, will you?"

"Great Whilloping Gradgenuzzlers! Never a dull moment," foretold Tarquin. . . . . and neither there was.

the end

WOOF!

Allan Ahlberg

Eric is a perfectly ordinary boy. Perfectly ordinary, that is, until the night when, safely tucked up in bed, he slowly turns into a dog! Fritz Wegner's drawings superbly illustrate this funny and exciting story.

VERA PRATT AND THE FALSE MOUSTACHES

Brough Girling

There were times when Wally Pratt wished his mum was more ordinary and not the fanatic mechanic she was; but when he and his friends find themselves caught up in a real 'cops and robbers' affair, he is more than glad to have his mum, Vera, to help them.

SADDLEBOTTOM

Dick King-Smith

Hilarious adventures of a Wessex Saddleback pig whose white saddle is in the wrong place, to the chagrin of his mother.

A TASTE OF BLACKBERRIES

Doris Buchanan Smith

The moving story about a young boy who has to come to terms with the tragic death of his best friend and the guilty feeling that he could somehow have saved him.